The Secret of Your Name
PROUD TO BE MÉTIS

Kiimooch ka shinikashooyen
AEN KISHCHITAYMOOK AEN LI MICHIF IWIK

David Bouchard
ART BY **Dennis J. Weber**
"MASTER OF THE METIS FIDDLE" **John Arcand**

Red Deer PRESS

FOREWORD FROM THE AUTHOR

Canada's Métis are the only mixed blood people in the world recognized by every level of government as being a nation. We Métis have our own language, flag, songs and stories. We have exciting traditions and a proud history.

Unfortunately, we have grown up in the aftermath of the resistance of 1885, an event often referred to in history books as the North West Rebellion. This was a sad period in Canadian history when Métis people, much like our First Nation cousins, were manipulated, deceived and robbed of our land, pride and culture.

Many of our grandparents were humiliated into denying their Native ties in favour of their more acceptable European bloodlines. They did whatever they could to appear white. My grandfather, born and raised Narcisse Beaudoin, died Nelson Bowdwin.

Today, many Métis are searching for the names of their grandmothers and grandfathers. Because European explorers and adventurers were usually men who took Native or country wives, we often speak of our grandmothers as being Native and our grandfathers as being European.

I am one whose grandmothers were Anishnaabe, Chippewa, Menominee and Innu.

I am one of many stepping forward to say that I am proud to be of mixed blood; that I am Proud to be Métis. This is for those who live my story.

And this is for all of our Grandmothers, our Kokums.

3

4

Lii Michif di Canada li moond maenlii, li goovarnimaan aen nishtawaynimaat enn Naasyoon. Niiyanaan lii Michif ni tipaytaenaan nutr laang, paviyoon, shaansoon pi lii zistwayr! Li taand kayaash kii kishchiitaytakwun aen ishi pimatishik pi enn bonn histwayr kii ayawuk lii vrae Michif.

Sid valeur, mishchet lii Michif kii nitawakiwuk apray nutr vyeu Michif ka kii notinikaychik an jis wit saan kaatr vaen saenk, ka shinikatayhk daan li Canada la Ribellyoon di Nor wes. Kii machipayinn aykooshpii aen kitimakuk daan listwayr di Canada poor lii Michif, tapishkoot lii pramyayr nasyoon, kii machaymikashoonaan, kii kayayshiwuk, kii kimotiwuk nutr terrain, aen kishchiitaymoyak pi ka kii ishi pimatishiyak kayash.

Mishchet lii Michif kii anwaytamuk aen li Michif ywichik nawut kii nootay li blaaniwiwuk ishpishchi wiiyawow. Ahpoo atith kii mooshoominaan pi ki nookoominaanik kii katawuk aen li michif iwichik. Pikoo ishi kii tootamuk chi li blaanwichik. Ni mooshoom aen nitawakit pi kii oopikiw Narcisse Beaudoin ki nipoo Nelson Bowdwin.

Anoosh mishchet lii Michif natonamuk okoomowawa pi omooshoomowawa taanshi shinikashoyit. Ayish lii gen di lootr borr pi li moond pikoyitae ka nidwatachik li piyii pikoo lii zomm lii famm di piyii kii ootinaywuk. Aykooshchi ki titwanaan ki kookoominaan oota ooshchi pi ki mooshoominaan lootr borr ooshchi. Maaka nimoo tapitow aykooshishi.

Niiya payek nookoomuk lii anishnabe, ojibwe, Menominee pi lii Innu.

Niiya paeyek ni niikaniin chi ytwayaan ni kishchiitaymoon li saan maylii aen ayayaan pi aen li Michif wiyaan. Oma li livr poor mishet li moond moon nistwayr ka pimatishichik. Pi oma miina poor ki kokoominanik.

Like many whose first fathers
Came from France in 1542
I somehow thought that I might be
A part of people much like you.

Like many whose first fathers
Sailed across the seas not knowing you
I somehow sensed I had the blood
Of people who were just like you.

Tapishkoot mishchet oopapayiwawa nishtum kii payototayew la Fraans
ooshchi an kaenz saan karaant deu
Gii itayten apootikwew niiya enn parsonn tapishkoot kiiya

Tapishkoot mishchet oopapayiwawa nishtum
Ka ki ashookaychik la merr aeka aen kishkaymishkik.
Nadow gii mooshitaan li saan aen ayayaan di moond tapishkoot kiiya.

7

But years and miles have washed away
All signs that should have led to you
Years and miles have hidden
All the clues that would have told of you.

Years and miles and people
Who are not like me and not like you
People in my life who knew
Who should have told the truth of you.

Maka lii zanii pi lii mill kii shipwaykotaewa
kakiyow lii siing kii paenatikooyen
Lii zaanii pi lii mill kii kashoowuk.
Kakiyow ka wapatayikooshiit kiiya ka kii mamishimik.

Lii zaanii pi lii mill pi li moond
Kaya tapishkoot niiya pi miina kiiya.
Li moond daan ma vii aen kii kishkaytakik
Awana la viritii chi kii achimish.

The secret of your name is out
I finally know my heritage.
It took me almost fifty years
To come to learn of you.

The secret's finally out
Of you my grandma, no, *my Nokum*
It's taken all these years
For me to come to learn the truth.

Kiimooch aen shinikashooyen kishkaytakwun.
Piiyish gishkayten taanday aen ooshchiyaan
Kaykaat saenkaant taan gii nootistaan
Chi kishkaytamaan awana kiiya.

Nimoo ayiwuk kiimooch kiiya
ooshchi kokoom mishchet lii
zaanii kii nootistanaan
Chi ki kishkaytamaan la vayritii.

I don't know where to start
I can only say *I'm sorry*
That no one ever spoke of you
That I was never told of you.

I don't know how to tell you
I can only say *I'm sorry*
That no one ever told me
That you were Anishnaabe.

12

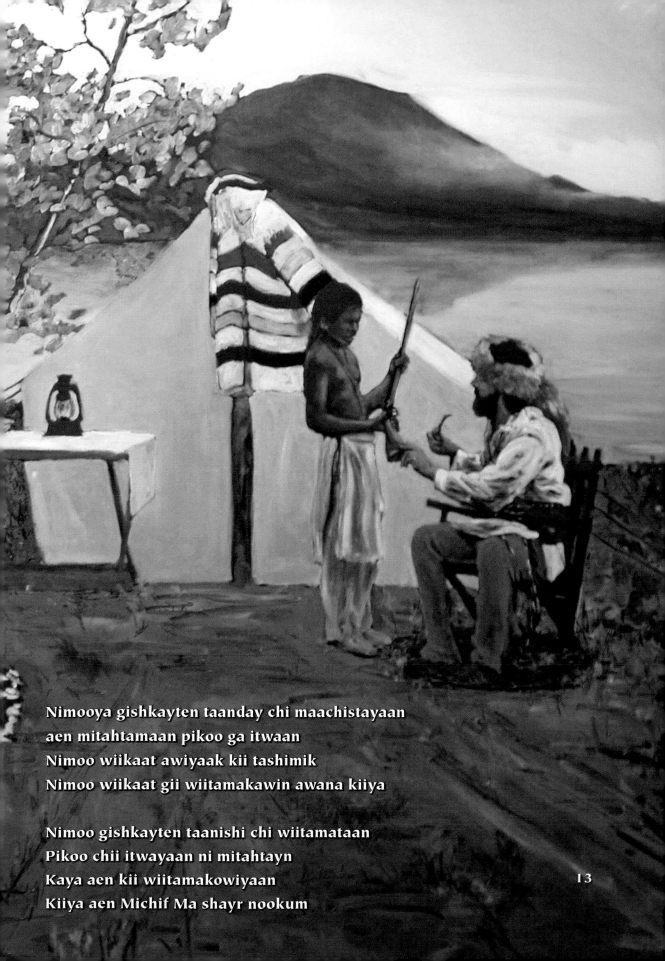

Nimooya gishkayten taanday chi maachistayaan
aen mitahtamaan pikoo ga itwaan
Nimoo wiikaat awiyaak kii tashimik
Nimoo wiikaat gii wiitamakawin awana kiiya

Nimoo gishkayten taanishi chi wiitamataan
Pikoo chii itwayaan ni mitahtayn
Kaya aen kii wiitamakowiyaan
Kiiya aen Michif Ma shayr nookum

13

Dear Nokum, I want you to know
It wasn't just your children.
Many, from good families too,
Did as your loved ones chose to do ...

They did not ever speak of you
Nor of a single person
Whose names would tell the world they knew
That you were Montagnais.

Dawayten chi kishkatamun nimooya
tii zaanfaan pikoo Mishet lii bonn famii miina
Anike ka shakihachik wiishtawow kii nashpitotakaewuk.

Nimoo wiikaat kii taashimikwuk maapoo enn paarsonn
Kaa shinikashoochik chi wiitamakayk daan li moond anchyii
aen Kishkaytakwuk aen Montagnais kiiya

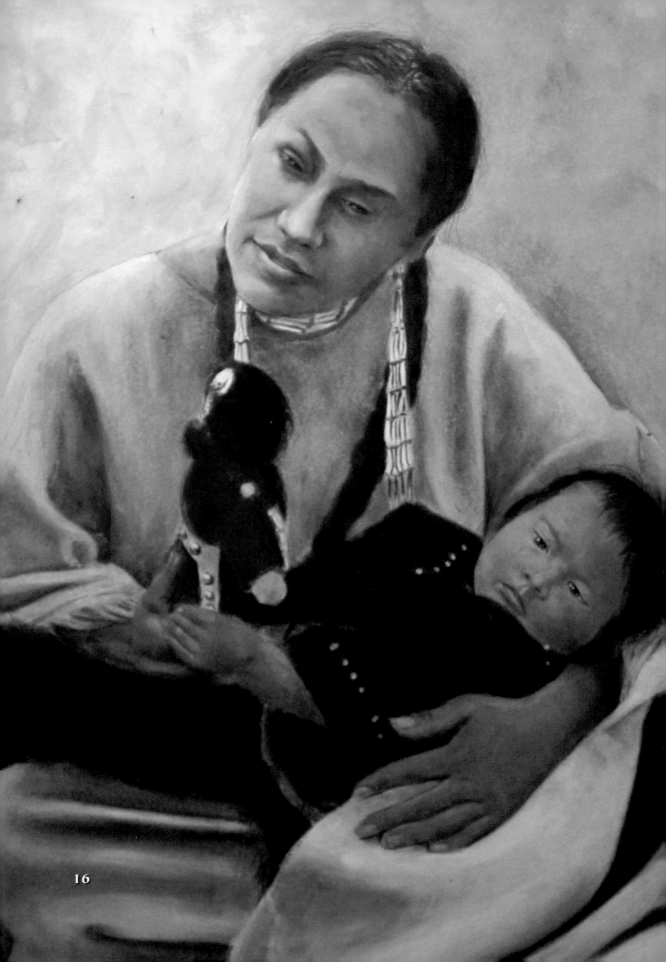

I'm sorry that I cannot sing
The songs that were passed down to you
The songs you heard your mother sing
The songs that I should own ...

I'm sorry but I cannot sing
I did not know so I did not learn
I have yet to hear a single song
Sung by a Chippewa ...

Ni mitaatayn ayka aen kaashkitayaan chi nakamooyaan.
Lii shaansoon ka kii miikashooyen
Lii shaansoon ka kii paytamun ki mamaan ka nakamoot.
Anihii chi kii tipaytamaan

Ni mitaatayn maaka nimoo gaashkitaan chi nakamooyaan.
Nimoo gii kishkaytayn akooshi nimoo
gii kaashkitaan chi kishkaytamaan.
Ni machayskwa enn shaansoon gii paytenn
Chi nakamoot an Chippewa

17

But I will go and seek them out
Then teach them to my children
I will go and find these songs
And claim them as my own.

And I'll sing them and I'll play my flutes
I will live my life to Honour you.
Our family too will come to learn
You were Menominee.

18

Maaka ga do natonen Ekooshpii ga kishkinamawawuk mii zaafaan
Ga doo mishken oohi lii shaansoon pi ga tipaytamashoon.

Ga nakamoon pi ga kitooshchikikaan moon flute
Ga pimatishin chi kishchitaymitaan
Nutr faamii wiishtawow ka pae kishkaytamuk
Kiiyawow Menominii

19

And Nokum – I am sad to say
I do not know your stories.
Not one has been passed down to me
Not one was ever told to me.

Nokum, I'm ashamed to say
I do not know your stories
The ones that you did surely tell
In hopes that I would hear.

20

Pi Nokoom sid valeur chi itwaeyaan
Nimoo gishkaytenn tii zistwayr
Nimoo ahpoo payek gii ooshchi nakatamakuk ahpoo
Nimoo ahpoo payek gii wii tamakawin.

Ma shayr Nokoom, nipaewishin chi itwaeyaan
Nimoo gishkayten tii zistwayr
Anihi ka kii shooshkwat itwaeyen
Kii li swaetiin chi paytamaan.

21

But I will go and seek them out
And claim them as my very own.
I will find then share them
So that others come to learn …

About the history of our family
Of our mothers and our fathers
Of the people I know nothing of
About the Algonquin …

Makaa ga doo mishken
Pi miina ga tipaytamashoon
Ga mishkenn pi ga taashkinenn
Aykooshi lii zootr ka kishkaytamuk

Chi achimook poor nutr famiiyinaan
Ki mamainaan pi ki papainaan
Li moond kaya aen kishkaymakik
Lii Algonkian

Dear Reader – I must now admit
That I hear her in my dreamtime
My Nokum tells me stories
About things I haven't lived

And when I wake I write them down
With caring and with passion
I scribe every word and sentence
Doing my best to Honour her ...

As I tell you this – through an open heart
I'm admitting to the source
Of my visions – of my stories
Every one inspired by her ...

Nimoo gaashkitaan kaya chi nakatwaytamaan
kiishpin kii kishkayten akooshishi chii shpayik.
Nimoo gaashkitaan kaya chi nakatwaytamaan …
Kii niipewykwuk chiin?

Obaen doon kii shiikatawaywuk une noovel naasyoon
Lii deu pramyayr Naasyoon nutr payii ooshchi?
Kii paypimatishin chiin aen kishchitaymooyen
Aen kii li Innu wiyen

25

I cannot help but wonder
Did you know that it would come to this?
I cannot help but wonder …
Did they make you feel ashamed?

Or did they bless a union
Of our country's two first nations?
Did you live your life with pride
Of having been Innu?

My quest has now begun – Thank God
I still have enough time to learn.
The customs and traditions
That you'd want for me to know.

That through song and dance and stories
I might come to know that which is mine.
Through memories you have taught me …
That I too am Ojibwe …

Machipayinn aen natonikayan
Gishkayten chi kiiwaeyaan kiishpin neu kiskayten
Kaayash ka kii pimatichiyak
Chi kishkaytamaan anima ka dawaytamun

Chi shapookishkaytamaan lii shaansoon pi lii daans pi lii zistwayr
Tadbaen ga paekishkayten kaykway ka tipaytamaan.
Aen ishi nakatwaytamaan kii kishkinamawin miina aen Ojibwe niiya

The secret of your name is out
I finally know my heritage
It has taken almost fifty years
To come to learn of you.

The secret's finally out
And now I know that *I am Métis*
And the world knows too, through all I do
How proud I am of you ...

Kiimootch ka shinikashooyen machi kishkaytakwun.
Piyish gishkayten Taanday ooshchiiyaan
Kaykaatch ni notistaan saenkaantaan chi pay kishkaymitaan.

Nimooywak kiimootchNi kishkayten aen li Michifiwiiyaan aekwa
Aen ishi mishaak li moond ni kishkaymikawin aen ishi pimatishiyaan
Taanshi aen ishi kishiitaymitaan.

PEOPLE, PLACES AND EVENTS

The **Algonquin** occupied immense territories in Ontario and in southern Québec. The Odawa, Ojibwe/Anishinaabe and the Cree are three Nations whose roots stem from the Algonquin culture.

The minuscule village of **Batoche** is the site in Saskatchewan where, in 1885, Louis Riel established the Métis provisional government and the Métis made their last stand. The Métis were defeated at Batoche, an event that marked the end of the resistance and put an end to the dreams of the Métis to establish an independent homeland in the North West. Gabriel Dumont fled to the U.S. Louis Riel turned himself over to Canadian authorities and was later hung.

The **Battle of Seven Oaks** took place in 1816 during the conflict between Canada's two rival fur trading companies, the Hudson's Bay and the North West Company. Dealing in pemmican was essential to the Métis way of life. To defend this right, the Métis were forced to take up arms. The Battle of Seven Oaks, won decisively by the Métis, was a key event in Métis history. The brutality of this battle had the effect of bringing about a quick end to a conflict that could have resulted in much more bloodshed. Métis and non-Métis lived peacefully thereafter in a culturally diverse Red River until the Red River Rebellion of 1869.

The Red River Métis lived by the **buffalo hunt**. The buffalo was the staple of Métis life. During the 1870s, hunts consisted of hundreds of hunters accompanied by their families on a uniquely versatile cart known as the Red River cart. It was only when American hunters, in their attempt to weaken the Aboriginal people, brutally slaughtered the buffalo until the buffalo disappeared. Along with the buffalo, the Métis way of life also disappeared.

The **Chippewa** are a people whose homeland is on the southern part of the Great Lakes. The word Chippewa originates from the word Ojibwe. It is used primarily in the U.S. while Anishinaabe is used in Canada.

The **Cree** Nation, whose homeland was central/western Canada, was closer to the French/Scottish newcomers than any other nation.

Fort Garry is the site where Louis Riel set up his first provisional government. It is here, in 1870, that the Red River Rebellion occurred.

This Métis uprising led to what would become the province of Manitoba. Fort Garry became Winnipeg, its capital.

Gabriel Dumont (page 4) was known as the Lord of the Plains and Captain of the Buffalo Hunt. Dumont is one of the principal characters in Métis history having served as Louis Riel's top strategist and lieutenant during the Resistance of 1885.

The **Hudson's Bay Company**, founded in 1670, played a major role in Canada's fur trade. The Company built a multitude of forts and outposts where Aboriginal people traded furs for commodities such as pots and blankets.

The **Innu** or **Montagnais** are a sub-group of the Algonquin Nation. Their traditional homeland lies in northern Québec and Labrador. For generations, the Innu lived as hunters and gatherers.

Kokum means Grandmother in Cree/Michif. **Nokum** means my Grandmother.

The **Lakota** are Native Americans, also known as Sioux. Today, they live mainly in North and South Dakota.

No one better represents or defines the rights of the Métis than **Louis Riel, Jr.** (page 26). Riel directed both the Red River Rebellion in 1860 and the North West Rebellion in 1885. Sir John A. Macdonald's government tried and executed Riel in 1885 on the grounds that he was a rebel and a traitor. He has since been pardoned and is now recognized as the Father of Manitoba.

The **Menominee** are a First Nations people whose homeland lies in the north eastern U.S. Today, they are found primarily in the state of Wisconsin.

Michif, the Métis language, is part French and part Cree.

The **Montagnais** are the largest indigenous group in Québec. They are more commonly known as Innu.

The **Ojibwe** or **Anishinaabe** survived by fishing, hunting and farming corn, squash and wild rice. Until the end of the 1700s, this powerful nation ruled immense territories in Canada and the northern U.S.

For my Kokums ... — D.B.

I'd like to dedicate the paintings in this book to my mother who grew up in Batoche, Saskatchewan. I think she was made ashamed of her culture and heritage, but since her death in 1991, the small things she instilled in me when she was alive have grown, not only into pride for the culture, but into a new identity. In *all* ways, I am now Metis. — D.J.W.

To all the Métis people. — J.A.

Text copyright © 2010 David Bouchard
Illustrations copyright © 2010 Dennis J. Weber AFCA CIPA
Music copyright © 2010 John Arcand CM

5 4 3 2 1

Published by
Red Deer Press
A Fitzhenry & Whiteside Company
www.reddeerpress.com

Michif translation by Norman Fleury
Cover and book design by Arifin Graham, Alaris Design
Sound mastering by Geoff Edwards – streamworks.ca
Printed and bound in Hong Kong, China

Acknowledgments
Financial support provided by the Canada Council,
and the Government of Canada through the Book Publishing
Industry Development Program (BPIDP).

THE CANADA COUNCIL | LE CONSEIL DES ARTS
FOR THE ARTS | DU CANADA
SINCE 1957 | DEPUIS 1957

Library and Archives Canada Cataloguing in Publication is available from the Library and Archives Canada
Library and Archives Canada Cataloguing in Publication
Bouchard, David, 1952–
        The secret of your name / David Bouchard ; illustrated by Dennis Weber.
Includes an audio CD.
Poems.
Music by John Arcand.
Text in English and Michif.
ISBN 978-0-88995-439-7
        I. Arcand, John II. Weber, Dennis III. Title.
PS8553.O759S43 2009   C811'.54   C2009-903069-1

United States Cataloguing-in-Publication Data
Bouchard, David.
        The secret of your name / David Bouchard ; illustrations by Dennis Weber ;
music by John Arcand.
[32] p. : col. ill. ; cm.
Includes CD recording.
Written in English and Michif.
Summary: The story of a person discovering their Metis heritage, and looking back over the culture and history of the Metis.
ISBN: 978-0-8899-5439-7 (pbk.)
1. Michif language — Juvenile fiction. 2. Métis — History — Juvenile fiction.
I. Title.
[E] dc22   PZ7.B683 2009